Disney
INFINITY

 Published in the United States by Random House Children's Books, a division of Random House LLC, 1745 Broadway, New York, NY 10019, and in Canada by Random House of Canada Limited, Toronto, Penguin Random House Companies. Random House and the colophon are registered trademarks of Random House LLC.

The term OMNIDROID is used by permission of Lucasfilm Ltd.

randomhousekids.com

For more information on Disney Infinity, please visit:
Disney.com/Infinity

ISBN 978-0-7364-3326-6 (trade)
ISBN 978-0-7364-8172-4 (lib. bdg.)

Printed in the United States of America

10 9 8 7 6 5 4 3 2 1

TOY BOX TROUBLE

By Amy Weingartner
Illustrated by Fabio Laguna and James Gallego

Random House New York

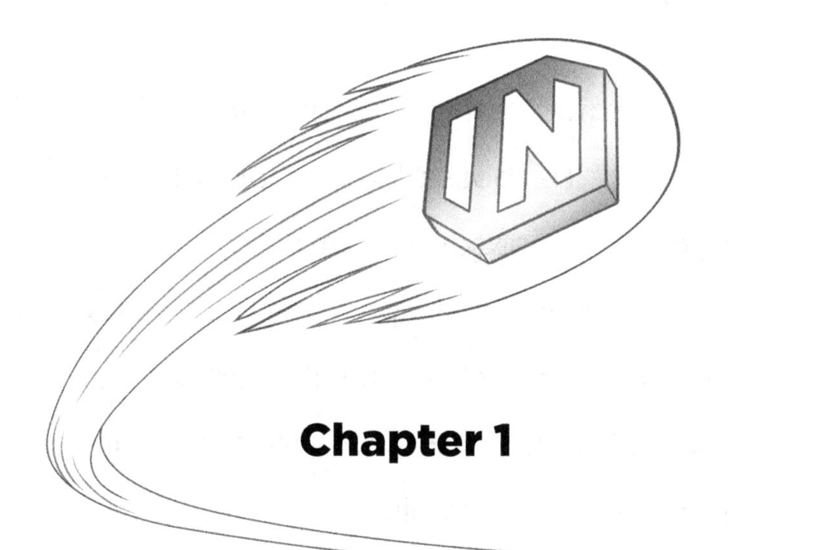

Chapter 1

Captain Jack Sparrow was resting after a long day. "Where *does* the time go?" he wondered aloud. He was lying in his favorite hammock on the deck of his ship. He watched the orange sun set over the sea.

After hours of fighting his pirate rival, Captain Barbossa, Jack thought he might just get some shut-eye.

Suddenly, a bright shooting star streaked across the sky. It sparkled like a gold doubloon. His nose for adventure twitched and told him to follow it. . . .

On the high seas, not far from Jack, Captain Barbossa ordered his crew to swab the decks.

"Ya lazy scurvies—keep it up!" Barbossa growled. He looked up into the dark night sky. He saw the same shooting star Jack was seeing, and a cold feeling came over him.

"What is that light?" he cried. He'd never seen anything like it! "It must be the work of some dark curse."

Barbossa paced the deck. Even though he was afraid of curses, he felt drawn to the star. It was a sign, like an X that marks the spot on a treasure map. And he couldn't resist treasure!

IN

It was evening in Metroville, and Dash, the super-fast kid Super, was ready to relax. Along with his Super family, the Incredibles, he had spent the day fighting the super villain Syndrome and his army of Omnidroids.

Dash looked up and saw a bright white light far off in the sky. It was a shooting star—but there was something strange about it.

"Hey, Violet," he called to his Super sister, "come here!"

"Wow," she said, "that's so cool!"

"Let's follow it!" Dash shouted.

Violet threw a force field around them. Running inside his sister's energy bubble, Dash used his super speed to propel them toward the star. . . .

Across Metroville, Syndrome fired up his rocket boots. He was practicing new moves with his upgraded super suit.

"I am so very awesome," he said. He broke into an evil laugh. *"Mwa-haaa-haaa!"*

Then the villain saw something unusual in the sky. It seemed to be a shooting star, but he'd never seen anything so . . . so . . . *nice*!

He wanted to follow it more than he wanted to crush Supers. And that was saying a lot, because Syndrome really liked crushing Supers.

In these different worlds—and in many others—something truly magical was happening in the light of the star.

And it was going to lead to something wonderful!

Chapter 2

With a sudden flash of light, Jack Sparrow and Barbossa found themselves standing together in a strange new landscape.

"Well, that was a curious sensation," Jack said, looking around at the flat green scenery. His nose twitched again.

"I knew it was a curse!" hissed Barbossa.

"And I see I am not alone," said Jack.

"You will never be rid of me, Jack Sparrow," the other pirate barked.

"I was talking about *them*!" Jack pointed to a spot across the open green space where three masked figures appeared in a sparkly glow. Dash, Violet, and Syndrome had all followed the same star . . . and arrived in the same place. Wherever this place was.

Barbossa ignored the newcomers. He drew his sword and attacked Jack.

"Feels like home already," said Jack,

dodging Barbossa's sword. He pulled out his own.

Barbossa and Jack fought until they reached the edge of a steep cliff. The pirate thrust his sword, but Jack parried. Barbossa lost his balance.

"I'll get you yet!" yelled Barbossa as Jack nudged him off the cliff.

"This is a wonderful land!" said Jack, happy to have finished off his rival. Something sparkled behind him. He turned around only to find Barbossa's cutlass pointed at him again!

"It is most wonderful indeed," hissed Barbossa.

"What kind of place is this, where

falling off a cliff doesn't get rid of a foe?" Jack asked, his eyes widening.

"A place where I will finally see the end of *you,* Jack Sparrow," whispered Barbossa.

Across the green terrain, yet another new arrival raced along the landscape. Vanellope von Schweetz was driving her Candy Kart as fast as she could. "That star sure has some sort of magical power," Vanellope said to herself. "I'm definitely not in *Sugar Rush* anymore!"

Suddenly, Dash came running by.

"Hey!" she called, and took off after him, down a nearby racing track. "Nobody's faster than me!"

"Don't feel bad," said a voice out of nowhere. Then a girl wearing the same

red suit as the fast boy materialized. "Nobody can beat my brother."

Vanellope screeched to a halt. "Whoa!" she said. "Who are you? Do you live here?"

Violet shook her head. "My brother and I just arrived. We saw this shooting star, and—"

"Me too!" Vanellope said.

"—it seemed to be telling us to go on an adventure!"

"Me too! I'm Vanellope, a racer from *Sugar Rush*."

"And my name is Violet," the Super girl answered. Then her brother raced back to them. "And this is Dash."

"Hey, so you were right, Vi," said Dash. "There's a huge castle over there. Let's explore it!"

Two other new arrivals to the strange land found themselves alone on the green field. Queen Elsa and Princess Anna of Arendelle had seen a shooting star from their castle window. For a moment, they had been mesmerized by its glow. Now they were . . . *here*!

Suddenly, Elsa and Anna heard a *whooshhhhh* overhead. An odd-looking man in a black-and-white suit and a cape flew overhead. He laughed maniacally as he raced into the distance.

"Where's he going?" asked Elsa.

Anna and Elsa watched Syndrome head toward a castle. Over the castle, a blue beacon lit up the sky.

"Let's go!" said Anna, adjusting her trusty shovel. "Maybe somebody there can tell us what's going on."

The sisters ran toward the castle. The closer they got, the more trees, rocks, and paths began to appear in the landscape. Then they saw more strangers coming toward them.

"Wait, you two!" a girl called. "That guy you're following is named

Syndrome. He is a *seriously* bad guy."

"Who are you?" asked Anna. She yelped as a boy ran up at super speed.

"I'm Violet," said the girl. "This is my brother Dash. We're used to dealing with Syndrome." Violet formed a pulsating plasma shield in her hand. "We're kind of *special.*"

"My sister, Elsa, is special, too," said Anna. Elsa had raised her arms. Frosty magic swirled around her hands as she formed a ball of ice and snow.

"And I have this!" Anna said, holding up her shovel.

"Cool," said Vanellope, arriving next to the group in her cart. "Can you make

a cherry snow cone for me?"

"I don't know how that star brought us here, but it seems like some of our enemies came with us," Violet said. "Are we up for the challenge?"

Meanwhile, Jack was sure he spotted something in the distance that looked like a castle. *Castles have walls. Big, strong walls,* Jack thought. *And I could use a few walls about now.*

Barbossa was chasing him—and getting closer!

"Look over there—treasure!" Jack yelled, hoping to trick the other pirate.

Treasure? Barbossa thought glee-fully, stopping to look where Jack was pointing. That gave Jack just enough time to make a run for the castle.

"Curse you, Jack Sparrow!" the villain shouted, stomping his foot. "Now, where did I put my pirate bombs?"

Chapter 3

Violet made herself invisible so that she could investigate the castle area first. She soon returned to her brother and their new friends.

"Wow, how did you do that so fast?" asked Anna as Violet became visible.

"Well, there's all kinds of really cool stuff in this world," Violet replied. "Like this space ranger jet pack. It just sort of appeared. I used it to fly into the sky and look around."

"What about Syndrome?" asked her brother.

"No sign of him," Violet said. "But I saw a couple of piratey-looking guys chasing each other."

"I want to fight a pirate," said Anna.

"Yeah . . . I mean, *arrrr!*" Vanellope said. "Fighting pirates sounds like fun. *Being* a pirate sounds like *more* fun!"

Dash pulled up to the group in a green, red, and white race car. "Sis is right. This place is like a big toy box. You just have to know how to find stuff. Anyone care to ride in style?"

Anna and Elsa had never seen a car before, but it looked exciting. They jumped in.

"But, Dash, you can't dri—" Violet began, but they were already speeding away. Vanellope followed in her cart. Violet strapped on the jet pack and flew after them.

When they reached the castle, Vanellope jumped out of her cart and ran up the stone stairs.

Dash yelled, "Hey, what are you doing?"

"Joining the pirate fight!" Vanellope called back as she disappeared into the castle.

"Wait!" said Dash, running up the castle stairs.

"Let's go," said Violet. She and Anna and Elsa ran after them.

They had just made it to the top of the stairs when a pirate jumped down from a parapet and landed in front of them. "Never fear—Captain Jack

Sparrow is here! I will save you from the dreaded Barbossa."

"How do we know you're not a bad guy?" asked Violet.

"I give you my word," he said, bowing deeply. "*And* I was here *first*."

They decided to trust the gentleman pirate. Jack led them to the turret, where they could get a view of the landscape. They saw what looked like an ocean in the distance.

"I assume that none of us knows where we are or exactly why we are here. So we need a plan," Jack said, putting a finger to his nose. "And the key to it is my pirate ship. It's here, too, somehow. I can *sense* that it's nearby."

"What's your point?" asked Anna.

"My ship can take us *anywhere*."

Before anyone could ask more questions, Barbossa and Vanellope raced up the stairs behind them! Vanellope was wearing a buccaneer's bandanna and brandishing a sword.

Barbossa's face was twisted into an ugly grin as he locked the door. "Welcome to *my* new headquarters. *You're trespassing.*"

"Yeah, trespassing," Vanellope said. "This castle is for pirates only."

Chapter 4

She looks so cool, Dash thought, watching pirate Vanellope leap into action. But he couldn't help asking, "Why are you with that guy?"

"Like I said, being a pirate sounds like fun," Vanellope replied.

Jack quickly surveyed the scene. The only way out seemed to be by plunging three levels down to the ground! Not good. Then he spotted a rope. It was just what they needed.

"Quick!" said Jack. "Ladies first!" Elsa nodded and knocked Barbossa off balance with a snowball. Then she grabbed Jack and jumped, swinging them to a lower level on the rope.

"Blast it!" shouted Barbossa. "He always gets away!"

"I got this," said Anna, and she threw her grappling hook to the opposite castle wall and swung to safety.

Violet created a plasma shield that

protected her and Dash. "Run!" she said. Her brother's super speed propelled them forward. They rolled past their enemies down a narrow ledge all the way down to the ground.

"We've got to go after them!" said Vanellope, unlocking the door and chasing them on foot. *"Arrrrr!"*

Barbossa was about to follow her when he heard a voice behind him. Syndrome appeared near the turret, riding on a hoverboard.

"I could help you defeat that problematic pirate," he said. "And you could help me crush those pint-sized Supers."

"I would like nothing more than to

bring Jack to his knees," admitted Barbossa.

"Kidnapping a princess just might help us get him right where we want him," said Syndrome slyly. "And those Supers, too."

"I've always wanted to kidnap a princess!" exclaimed Barbossa.

"Ha, ha, ha! Then jump aboard!" Syndrome said gleefully.

Barbossa and Syndrome chased

their rivals. They caught up with them at the far edge of the castle grounds and attacked. The two villains forced the heroes back toward the castle.

Violet, Dash, Jack, Elsa, and Anna worked together to fend off Barbossa and Syndrome. Violet and Dash took care of Syndrome's zero-point energy attacks, while Anna used her shovel to block Vanellope's playful sword blows. Barbossa kept Jack busy in a duel that moved around to the edge of the moat.

The castle had many bridges, walls, and levels. The team discovered that certain movements allowed them to move faster or better. They could jump extra high if they wanted to climb onto something or were backed into a corner. And they could use tools and toys that just seemed to be part of this Toy Box world.

Elsa found a slingshot and fired. "Take that!" she yelled triumphantly, hitting Barbossa.

"Back at you!" Vanellope and Barbossa said, tossing a cherry bomb at her and the Incredibles.

In the smoke, Syndrome disappeared from the fight. Violet and Dash knew he was up to something. But for the moment, they had to help Jack, Anna, and Elsa fend off the attacks coming from Barbossa and Vanellope.

"I still can't understand why you're fighting with *them*!" Dash said to Vanellope.

"I kind of like good bad guys!" she shouted back. "And Barbossa is a good bad guy . . . like an old friend of mine."

Syndrome reappeared on his hoverboard and swooped down.

"Watch out!" said Dash.

The villain quickly zoomed in and pulled Anna onto his hoverboard.

"Anna!" Elsa shouted, firing her slingshot at Syndrome. "Let go of my sister!"

"Unhand her!" Jack added. But it

was too late. Syndrome was already fleeing into the sky with Anna!

"Next I'm taking your ship!" he called as he zoomed away.

"Get back here!" Barbossa shouted from the castle wall. "That was not the plan! You double-crossing, princess-stealing, low-down—"

"Whoa, wait a second—'double-crossing'?" Vanellope said, suddenly suspicious. "You were going to kidnap Anna? That is *not* what I signed up for! I quit!" She threw her sword and pirate bandanna to the ground.

She stomped on Barbossa's toe. The pirate teetered at the edge of the

castle wall, hopping on one foot.

Not again, he thought, grabbing Vanellope as he fell.

"You guys rescue Vanellope and take care of Barbossa," said Violet. "I'll go after Syndrome. He's one bad guy I *know*!"

"Agreed," said Jack. "And do not fail. If you don't find him, *we may never see fair Anna again.*"

Chapter 5

Hanging by the tips of his fingers from the edge of the castle wall, Barbossa dangled Vanellope over the castle's moat from two levels up. She concentrated, trying to use her glitch power. It allowed her to teleport short distances and even through solid objects. Unfortunately, it didn't always work. Glitching was glitchy!

"Oh, sour tarts," she grumbled.

"Put her down right now!" said Jack from below.

"As you wish," said Barbossa. He dropped Vanellope, and she landed in the moat with a splash.

"Hey, that was too close!" she called up, spitting out water. "You almost missed the moat. I could have been hurt!"

"I wasn't aiming for the water," the pirate hissed. Then he turned to Jack. "Listen to me, Sparrow. I want to make

that double-crossing redheaded rogue walk the plank. *You* want the princess back. What do you say? Partners?"

"You can't trust him!" said Vanellope.

"True. But . . ." Jack began to pace, deep in thought. "No tricks?" he asked Barbossa.

"You have my word."

"I'll need more than that!" said Jack.

Barbossa pulled out a shiny gold doubloon and tossed it to Jack. Jack looked at it closely and nodded.

"Consider that my guarantee," said Barbossa. "I get it back if we succeed."

"All right. Partners," Jack said, throwing the other pirate a rope.

Jack and Dash searched the grounds for anything useful. They found toys, bombs, blasters, and gadgets of all sorts that this Toy Box world seemed to offer.

In the castle stable, Jack mounted a magnificent horse, and Dash discovered a carriage with large monster-truck wheels.

"Yes!" Dash said, jumping in the driver's seat and revving the engine.

They returned to discover that Barbossa had found a horse of his own. He set off after Syndrome.

Violet flew ahead of them, using the jet pack.

The stakes were high. They had to get to the *Black Ship* before Syndrome took it and disappeared with Anna . . . *forever!*

Chapter 6

The group hurried in the direction Syndrome had flown. Soon they saw another glowing blue beacon lighting up the sky. When they got closer, they could see that the blue light was hovering over a small village harbor—and best of all, there was Jack's ship!

"It could be a trap," said Jack, boarding the *Black Ship* first. The team searched everywhere—no Anna.

But Violet found something else. "There's a whole village here," she said. "Anna could be hidden anywhere!"

"Where's Barbossa?" Dash asked.

"He said, 'If there be a pirate village, then there be pirates,'" Violet told them, imitating Barbossa's gravelly voice. "Then he ran off."

"If Syndrome figures out all the daft stuff that this world has to offer, he just might find a way to build an army of . . ." Jack searched for the word.

"Omnidroids!" Dash shouted.

"And that would be bad," Violet added matter-of-factly.

"Very," Jack said.

"Right you are!" Syndrome said, suddenly whizzing overhead on his hoverboard.

"Watch out!" Jack shouted, whipping out the blaster he had found in the stable.

"The princess is nearby, but *where,* you'll never find out!" Syndrome shouted. "This place is full of surprises. Did you know that I was able to find everything I needed to create a new Omnidroid army? And the best part is that it will be arriving in"—he looked at his watch—"two minutes. And man, oh, man, is it going to *crush* you!"

With a villainous laugh, he flew off.

"Prepare for battle!" Jack warned the team. Dash and Violet were ready, but the others didn't know what to expect from the Omnidroids.

Soon enough, the ground started shaking. The first wave was attacking! The robots were huge, with metal arms and legs. They marched through the village with their arms spinning, smashing anything in their way. They had sharp claws on their robot arms that sliced through trees.

"Fight!" Jack said, leading the charge into battle.

Elsa threw snowballs at the robots. The droids just shook them off.

Violet's plasma shield began to fail under the robots' crushing blows.

A second wave of droids dropped from the sky. Jack's blaster attacks worked on some of them. But other robots were getting closer. *If Barbossa shows up,* Jack thought, *we might have a chance. . . .*

In the village, Vanellope and Dash could hear the blasts. They were searching every building when they discovered Anna in a jail cell!

"Anna!" cried Vanellope.

"Vanellope? Dash? I was waiting for you guys to get here!"

"Waiting?" Vanellope asked.

Dash ran off to search the building at super speed for the key.

"Syndrome laughed at my shovel for being low-tech, and he left it with me," Anna said. "I was waiting until you got here to do this!"

She smashed the lock with a mighty blow of her shovel!

"Cool," Dash said, returning too late with the key. "With shovel power like that, you could be a Super in Metroville!"

Anna smiled at the thought. "Let's go get Syndrome."

Dash, Vanellope, and Anna dodged the Omnidroid attacks while they made their way to the harbor. Dash used his super speed to zip back and forth, which confused the metal monsters. Vanellope glitched in and out of the action, tripping the robots. And Anna whacked several of the metal monsters with her shovel.

Elsa ran to her sister and hugged her, then quickly filled her in. "We have to be very careful," Elsa warned. "This battle is *far* from over."

Armed with blasters, Jack and

Violet were still in the middle of the battle with the Omnidroids, but they cheered when they saw that Anna was safe. Vanellope joined the fight, tossing cherry bombs at the Omnidroids.

Syndrome returned, leading another wave of robots. One of them blasted a hole right through the captain's cabin on Jack's ship.

"Villain!" Jack yelled at Syndrome.

"Oh, did your precious *Black Ship* get a boo-boo?" Syndrome was flying overhead, surveying the damage. "Goodbye, Jack Sparrow! You got your princess back just in time to be defeated. Fire cannons!"

"Did somebody say 'cannons'?" shouted a familiar voice.

Barbossa had arrived on a rowboat. Dozens more rowboats filled with pirates were behind him. And the pirates had plenty of pirate bombs and cannons!

"I never thought I would be glad to see *your* face!" Jack shouted merrily to his old rival. "Where did you find this motley crew?"

"I've learned a little something about this strange land," Barbossa called to Jack. "Seems that if you've got some coins, you can find some friends."

"Friends with cannons are the best kind!" Jack called back.

"Indeed!" replied Barbossa, giving his crew the signal to open fire. Some of the pirates fired from their boats. Others quickly brought cannons ashore and found positions to attack.

When Syndrome saw what Barbossa and the pirates were doing, he was *not* happy. The cannon fire coming from the pirates was knocking down his Omnidroids! Robot parts and claws were piled up and scattered on the ground.

Luckily, a handful of his Omnidroids had taken over the *Black Ship*. Now Syndrome *knew* he was going to win . . . and that made him *very* happy!

Just then, Vanellope threw a cherry bomb that destroyed one of the Omnidroids. In the middle of the dust, smoke, and destruction, she saw a magical glittery swirl of light. Out of the light stepped a huge figure that she recognized immediately.

Just in time, she thought.

"Ralph!" she called. "My main man! I've got a job that's just right for someone of your talents."

Jack and Barbossa were at the dock, firing cannons at Syndrome. Anna, Elsa, Dash, and Violet were retreating from the ship and heading back to the dock. Vanellope ran to them with her big friend in brown overalls. He raised his oversized fists above the head of an approaching Omnidroid.

"I'm Ralph," he bellowed. "I'm going to wreck it!"

"Do it, big guy!" shouted Vanellope.

Violet, Elsa, and Anna watched wide-eyed while Ralph smashed all of

Syndrome's Omnidroids! One. Two. Three. Four. He wrecked them with ease.

"My dad would *love* this guy!" Dash cheered.

"My Omnidroids! I don't understand! They're indestructible," wailed Syndrome.

"Don't cry, ya big baby," said Vanellope.

Syndrome unleashed an energy blast to destroy Vanellope, but Ralph blocked the crackling bolt. Ready to wreck it, Ralph grabbed the hoverboard. He spun the hoverboard in the air and threw it to the ground.

Syndrome tried to get up, but Ralph quickly pinned him with his big bare foot.

"What's that smell?" Vanellope leaned over and sniffed next to the villain's head. "It's the smell of de-*feet.* HA!"

Chapter 7

"Victory is mine," Barbossa said smugly. "Thanks to *me*."

"It was really more of a group effort," Jack replied. His ship rocked in the town harbor.

"True. You helped," Barbossa said.

"Hey, you two," Anna interrupted, "do you really think we can get back home on your ship?"

"My ship can get us anywh—"

"Look, everyone!" Dash said, pointing to the sky. "A shooting star."

Above the masts of the great *Black Ship,* a shooting star blazed. Violet and Dash saw it. Jack saw it. Elsa and Anna saw it. Barbossa saw it. They could all feel its magic.

"What star? I didn't see it!" said Vanellope, running onto the deck. "I was taking a licorice break!"

"It'll be back," said Dash. "It's fast, like you."

"No, fast like *you,*" said Vanellope, hitting him on the shoulder.

"Send me to Davy Jones's locker if I have to listen to this kind of nonsense!" growled Barbossa.

"No need to worry," Jack said jauntily. "Seems our adventures here are at an end."

They all felt a magical power begin to pull at them.

"We're going home, aren't we?" said Anna. "We'll miss you, Jack."

"Goodbye, fair maidens and Incredible family," said Jack as he bowed to everyone on the team. "To future adventures!"

He turned to Barbossa, and the two pirates immediately began arguing about which way to go to follow the star.

"Goodbye, everyone," said Elsa. "Thank you for saving my sister."

Violet scanned the sky. "Well, I guess this is our turn. See that star? That one leads us home. Let's go."

"Do we have to bring Syndrome back to Metroville?" Dash moaned.

"All right, Ralphy," said Vanellope, jumping onto one of Ralph's shoulders. "Let's grab the next star home."

"Nice to meet you folks," Ralph said, giving them a friendly wave.

"Look up!" Dash said.

Vanellope saw a shooting star and smiled. "Okay, I see it. That's our star! This train is bound for *Sugar Rush*!"

The good guys promised to reunite and have more adventures in this wonderful world—a fascinating place that seemed more exciting now that they knew it better.

Syndrome grumbled crossly under his breath that he'd be back, too. No one paid attention to him, and that made him very crabby.

Suddenly, everything around them began to sparkle.

Soon only Jack and Barbossa were left—and they were still bickering.

Before catching their star home, Jack saw something moving toward them. It appeared to be a large, hairy blue monster with some kind of green eyeball on legs walking alongside him.

Barbossa said to Jack, "Remember, just because I helped you once, that does not mean I will ever do it again."

"Never say never," said Jack, wagging his finger knowingly.

The eyeball called to them, "Hey, hey, pirates! Over here! You're just the types we're looking for. I have a treasure map! See? Check this out! We have a map, and you guys are pirates. This is perfect! It's a match made in heaven. Speaking of heaven, did you see that star? Crazy, huh? Where are we? Never mind. What do you say we team up and search for treasure?"

Jack looked at Barbossa and raised an eyebrow.

"Well," said Barbossa, "maybe we can throw in our lot together just *one more time*."

The eyeball guy kept talking. "How about it? Huh? I'm Mike. This is Sulley. What do you guys say?"

"It *is* treasure we're talking about, after all," Jack replied.

He and Barbossa smiled and turned to greet their new friends. . . .

THE END?